12 ARTISTS WHO CHANGED THE WORLD

by Allan Morey

12 STORY LIBRARY
MORE TO EXPLORE

www.12StoryLibrary.com

12-Story Library is an imprint of Bookstaves.

Photographs ©: Marc Vorwerk/Alamy Stock Photo, cover, 1; PD, 4; SIAATH/Shutterstock.com, 5; PD, 6; PD, 7; Nadar/PD, 8; PD, 9; Joseph Durand-Ruel/PD, 10; Art Institute of Chicago/PD, 11; Alfred Stieglitz/CC1.0, 12; High Museum of Art, Atlanta/PD, 13; PD, 13; Argentina. Revista Vea y Lea/PD, 14; PD, 15; Guillermo Kalho/PD, 16; JENS KALAENE/Alamy Stock Photo, 17; Science History Images/Alamy Stock Photo, 18; Rana Royalty free/Alamy Stock Photo, 19; Laurent Koffel/Shutterstock.com, 20; 360b/Shutterstock.com, 21; ines s./CC2.0, 21; Adrian Piper/CC3.0, 22; David Campos/MACBA/CC3.0, 23; Karen Petersen/Alamy Stock Photo, 24; photocritical/Shutterstock.com, 25; Uli Deck/Associated Press, 26; Matt Brown/CC2.0, 27; PD, 28; Sharon Mollerus/CC2.0, 29

ISBN
9781632357137 (hardcover)
9781632358226 (paperback)
9781645820017 (ebook)

Library of Congress Control Number: 2019938659

Printed in the United States of America
July 2019

About the Cover

Ai Weiwei in Berlin in 2015.

Access free, up-to-date content on this topic plus a full digital version of this book. Scan the QR code on page 31 or use your school's login at 12StoryLibrary.com.

Table of Contents

1

Leonardo da Vinci: True Renaissance Man

Leonard da Vinci is best known for his painting *Mona Lisa*. This portrait of a smiling woman has been seen on everything from posters to memes. With his masterpiece, da Vinci created a strange optical illusion. People who see her in person feel *Mona Lisa* is looking at them, no matter where they stand.

Da Vinci was born in Italy in 1452. He lived during the Renaissance. This was a period of great advancements in the arts and sciences. To paint *The Last Supper*, da Vinci used a new technique developed during this time. Earlier paintings often looked flat. They did not have depth. *The Last Supper* used perspective. Objects in the background looked smaller. This created a scene people felt they could step right into.

Da Vinci was more than just an artist. He was a scientist. He studied subjects like anatomy. He

THINK ABOUT IT

Leonardo da Vinci studied anatomy. He wanted to learn how the body worked. How might this help an artist?

14

Leonardo Da Vinci's age when he was apprenticed to study art

- Da Vinci was left-handed and used mirror writing. His notes were written backwards but could be read when seen in a mirror.
- He had an idea for a flying machine called an ornithopter. It would use mechanical wings that flapped.
- *Mona Lisa* is on display at the Louvre Museum in Paris, France.

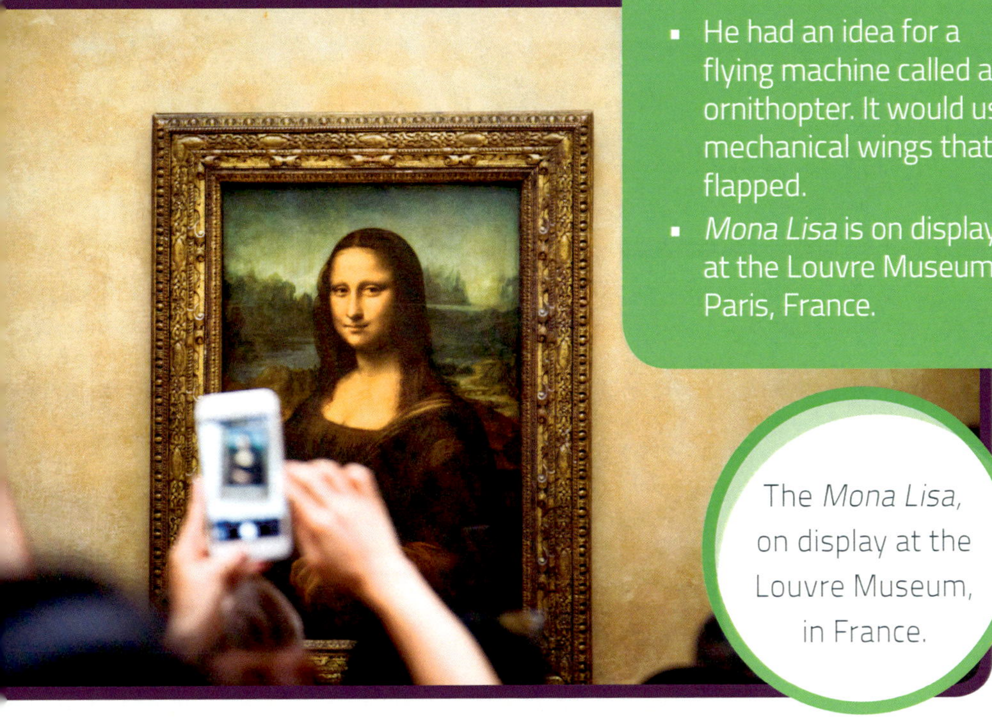

The *Mona Lisa,* on display at the Louvre Museum, in France.

learned how body parts work. Da Vinci was also an inventor. In his notes, he drew sketches of many ideas. They included flying machines and armored vehicles.

Da Vinci died in 1519. Sketches of his ideas have helped inspire modern-day inventions. Today, airplanes and tanks are a reality.

2 Élisabeth Vigée Le Brun: Royal Portraits

Le Brun painted this self-portrait in 1782.

Before the 1700s, there were few successful female artists. Art schools did not like to accept them as students. Women had a difficult time getting training. Also, people did not value what women created. They did not think women could produce fine art. Marie-Louise Élisabeth Vigée Le Brun helped change people's opinions.

Le Brun was born in 1755 in Paris, France. From an early age, she liked to draw. Her father was also an artist. He encouraged her to paint. But after his death, Le Brun mostly had to teach herself.

Le Brun became a gifted portrait artist. She had an ability to make people look elegant and relaxed in her paintings. People all over France admired her work. Rich nobles hired her to paint their portraits. Even the Queen of France, Marie Antoinette, wanted to sit for Le Brun. The artist painted more than 20 portraits of the queen.

Le Brun died in 1842. She is considered the most gifted portrait painter of her time.

A portrait of Marie Antoinette painted by the artist in 1783.

1779

Year when Élisabeth Vigée Le Brun first painted Marie Antoinette

- Le Brun earned a living by painting portraits of people.
- She also painted many self-portraits. She had to view herself in a mirror as she worked on these paintings.
- She created more than 600 paintings.

HAVING A PORTRAIT PAINTED

Before the 1800s, people did not have cameras. They could not take selfies. If they wanted a picture of themselves, they had to hire an artist. The artist would then paint their portrait. Sitting for a portrait was not easy. People had to stay still for hours at a time as the artist worked. It could take days or weeks to complete a portrait. Some portraits took artists years to paint.

3

Claude Monet: Making an Impression

Claude Monet was a French painter born in 1840. He grew up along the northern coast of France. As a child, he had a love for ships and liked to draw them.

Some of Monet's early sketches impressed painter Eugène Boudin. He convinced the young artist to try landscape painting. At the time, most artists painted outdoor scenes while in their studios. They worked from memory. Boudin was a plein air painter. Plein air means "open air." Boudin worked outdoors, directly observing what he painted.

Claude Monet in 1898.

25

Number of paintings in Monet's haystack series

- In his teens, Monet drew caricatures of his friends and teachers.
- His water lily paintings were of the pond in his garden.
- Camille Pissarro, Paul Cézanne, and Edgar Degas are other famous impressionist painters.

This painting from Monet's haystack series was done in 1891.

Painting outdoors helped Monet notice how colors and shadows changed throughout the day. This was also true from season to season. He would paint the same subject over and over again to show these changes. His haystack series is one example. His many haystack paintings all look different. They were painted at different times of the day and the year.

Before Monet's time, most paintings were realistic. Artists wanted their work to imitate real life. But in 1874, Monet helped bring about a new idea in art. His painting *Impression, Sunrise* was of a French harbor on a hazy morning. But Monet did not paint the scene exactly as it looked. Rather, he painted his impression, or idea, of it. The ships in the background are simply gray. The waves in the water are shown with thick brushstrokes. The sun is a bright orange ball. This new style of painting was called impressionism.

Monet died in 1926. He is best known for his impressionist paintings of water lilies.

4

Mary Cassatt: Proving Americans Can Paint

Mary Cassatt was an American painter born in 1844. She grew up during a time when women were not encouraged to be artists. Few art schools accepted them as students. Cassatt also lived when American artists had little respect. Art critics felt they knew little of art and culture.

Cassatt did not let people's opinions about women or Americans stop her. She moved to Europe to study art. She taught herself how to paint by copying the masterpieces she saw in museums. In 1868, her hard work paid off. Cassatt's painting *The Mandolin Player* was displayed at an art gallery in Paris.

In 1877, Cassatt met Edgar Degas. He was part of the impressionist art movement. Impressionists often used bright colors. They did not worry about painting lifelike images. Degas asked Cassatt to exhibit her art with other impressionists. She was the only American to join this group of artists.

Mary Cassatt (left) in 1910.

Cassatt painted *The Child's Bath* in 1893.

21

Mary Cassatt's age when she moved to Paris, France, to study art

- Along with paintings, Cassatt created etchings. These are pictures made on metal plates.
- She did not paint landscapes, like most other impressionists. She painted indoor scenes.
- She liked to paint people doing everyday things, from drinking tea to reading the newspaper.

Cassatt died in 1926. She is best known for her paintings of mothers and their children. She wanted to show the love they shared.

IMPRESSIONISM

The impressionist art movement began in the late 1800s. It started with French painters like Claude Monet and Edgar Degas. Before this period, artists painted realistic images. But impressionists wanted to show how something looked at a quick glance. To do this, they used loose brushstrokes. Their brushstrokes were not blended into the painting. Up close, their paintings often look blurry. But from a distance, a picture can be clearly seen.

5

Georgia O'Keeffe: Experimenting with Abstract Art

American painter Georgia O'Keeffe was born in 1887. She grew up on a dairy farm in southern Wisconsin. From an early age, she liked to draw. O'Keeffe studied art at the Art Institute of Chicago. Afterward, she went to the Art Students League in New York. At these schools, she learned realistic painting. In paintings like *Untitled (Dead Rabbit with Copper Pot)*, her work showed lifelike images.

O'Keeffe was not satisfied to simply paint realistic scenes. She wanted to express feelings and ideas in her work. In 1915, she created several charcoal drawings. They were experiments in abstract art. They were not realistic representations of anything. They mostly showed shapes and curved lines that O'Keeffe saw in nature.

Nature would play a big part in O'Keeffe's work. In the 1920s, she began to paint large close-ups of flowers. Oftentimes, these were flowers she planted in her garden, like petunias. But perhaps her best-known painting is *Black Iris*. O'Keeffe also painted images of animal bones she found in the deserts of New Mexico.

O'Keeffe died in 1986. Today she is remembered as one of America's first abstract artists.

O'Keeffe in 1933.

291

Name of the art gallery in New York that first exhibited Georgia O'Keeffe's charcoal drawings

- In 1942, O'Keeffe married Alfred Stieglitz, owner of the 291 Gallery.
- She painted landscapes of places she lived. These included New York City and New Mexico.
- The Georgia O'Keeffe Museum is in Santé Fe, New Mexico. It has nearly 1,000 pieces of O'Keeffe's art.

O'Keeffe's *Red Canna* was painted in 1919.

MODERNISM

The modernist art movement lasted from the late 1800s to the early 1940s. At the time, many artists were not concerned with showing lifelike images in their art. Their work was abstract. Sometimes, they used colors to capture emotions. Or they used shapes to hint at the meaning of their work.

6

Pablo Picasso: Master of Many Styles

Picasso in 1962.

Pablo Ruiz Picasso was a Spanish artist born in 1881. He was a painter and sculptor. During his lifetime, he created thousands of pieces. Picasso is best known for his unique styles. His Blue Period began about 1901. Paintings from this period, such as *The Old Guitarist*, used many shades of blue. Their color made the figures look sad and frail.

About 1909, Picasso experimented with a style known as cubism. In these paintings, objects were often reduced to simple shapes. In portraits, faces might look like their features had been chopped up and moved around. They might have both eyes on the same side of their face. Their nose might be in an odd place.

Picasso also created some amazing sculptures. Many of them were found-object pieces. Picasso would take things he found and turn them into works of art. He made *Bull's Head* out of a bike seat and handlebars. *Baboon and Young* used one of his son's toy cars.

Picasso died in 1973. His unique styles changed the way people look at art. They also influenced how many artists create art today.

1937

Year when Picasso finished *Guernica*, one of his most famous paintings

- In *Guernica*, people and animals look like they are suffering. This painting shows the tragedy of war.
- Picasso also had a Rose Period, when he painted with shades of red.
- The Museu Picasso in Barcelona, Spain, shows thousands of Picasso's works.

The Old Guitarist was painted between late 1903 and early 1904.

THINK ABOUT IT

Like Picasso, many artists draw, paint, and sculpt. They also create art using different styles. How might trying different types and styles of art help an artist?

7

Frida Kahlo: Her Talent Was No Accident

Frida Kahlo de Rivera was a Mexican painter. She was born in 1907. In a way, Kahlo became an artist by accident. As a teen, she was in a serious bus crash. Her spine was fractured in many places. She suffered broken bones throughout her body. As she recovered from her injuries, she studied art.

Frida Kahlo in 1932.

1929

Year when Frida Kahlo married artist Diego Rivera

- Self-portraits Kahlo painted after meeting Rivera often show her wearing traditional dress.
- Kahlo painted *The Two Fridas* after she divorced Rivera. One Frida is shown as a traditional woman. The other is a modern woman.
- In 2002, the movie *Frida* was released about Kahlo's life. Salma Hayek starred as the artist.

Kahlo's early suffering would stay with her throughout her life. It also showed up in her paintings. *The*

Broken Column shows her with a crumbling column for a spine. Pain from her accident sometimes made it difficult for her to work.

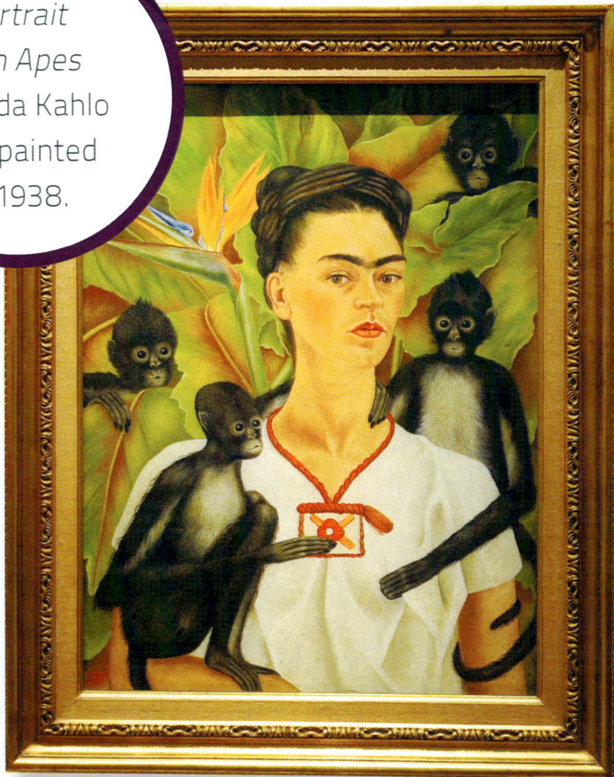

Portrait with Apes by Frida Kahlo was painted in 1938.

Kahlo's work was often a mix of realism and abstract art. She would paint a lifelike portrait of herself. But she might have exotic animals in the background. Or she might be wearing a necklace of thorns. Her style could be somewhat surrealistic. An example is her painting *Root*. In it, the artist is lying on the ground. Roots sprout from her chest and stomach. This painting showed Kahlo's desire to support life. She wanted to be a mother but never had children.

Kahlo died in 1954. She is best known for her many self-portraits.

SURREALISM

The surrealist art movement began in the early 1900s. Surrealists created highly imaginative works of art. The images they painted were strange and fantastic. They wanted their art to have a dreamlike quality. Salvador Dali is one of the best-known surrealists. His masterpiece *The Persistence of Memory* shows clocks that look like they are melting.

8

Andy Warhol: Making Pop Art Popular

Andrew Warhola was born in 1928 in Pittsburgh, Pennsylvania. He is better known as Andy Warhol. He was a pop artist and a filmmaker.

Warhol studied art at what is now Carnegie Mellon University. After graduating, he worked as a commercial illustrator. He made drawings for advertisements and magazines. But he dreamed of becoming an artist.

Warhol began seriously painting in the 1950s. But he was not fond of the leading art movement in the United States. It was called abstract expressionism. Some of these paintings were dripped paint on canvas. Others showed large splashes of color. Warhol wanted to show real images in his work.

Beginning in the early 1960s, Warhol began to paint everyday objects. He painted Campbell's soup cans and Coke bottles. He also painted boxes of Brillo soap pads. His time as a commercial illustrator helped with these works of art. Warhol had learned how to

Warhol's 32 *Campbell's Soup Cans* paintings (1962) are in the Museum of Modern Art in New York.

32

Number of different soup cans Andy Warhol painted

- Warhol created a series of paint-by-numbers paintings. They included *Do It Yourself (Seascape)* and *Do It Yourself (Flowers)*.
- In the 1960s and 1970s, he produced several underground movies. These experimental movies were not shown in big movie theaters.
- The Andy Warhol Museum is in his hometown of Pittsburgh, Pennsylvania.

create recognizable and attention-grabbing images.

Warhol's style of art was called pop art. It originally began in the 1950s in the United Kingdom. But artists like Warhol made it popular in the United States. Pop art was often bright, bold, and simple. It took everyday objects and portraits of famous people and turned them into fine art.

Andy Warhol died in 1987. He is remembered for painting Campbell's soup cans. But he also created prints of stars like Marilyn Monroe.

9 Ai Weiwei: Artist and Activist

Ai Weiwei was born in China in 1957. He is a painter, sculptor, photographer, and filmmaker. He is also a social activist. Ai grew up during China's Cultural Revolution. During this time, the Communist Party wanted to control all aspects of life in the country. Old traditions were destroyed as the government sought to modernize the nation. Artists were limited in the types of art they could create. And their art needed to serve the people. It could not criticize the government.

From an early age, Ai was interested in art. But he felt the government put too many restrictions on what artists could create. So in 1981, Ai moved to New York City. There, he went to art school.

Ai soon began to produce paintings and sculptures. Profile of Marcel Duchamp in a Coat Hanger was one of his early works. It honored Marcel Duchamp. This French artist believed everyday objects could be turned into art. Ai also had a talent for combining the traditional and modern in his work. He would find old Chinese vases. Then he painted the Coca-Cola logo on them.

Much of Ai's later work comments on social issues. In 2016, he placed thousands of life vests around the columns of a concert hall in Berlin, Germany. He wanted to draw attention to the crisis of refugees.

Weiwei's life vest art installation in Berlin drew attention to the refugee crisis.

9,000

Number of children's backpacks used in Ai Weiwei's sculpture *Remembering*

- *Remembering* honors the children who died from a 2008 earthquake in China.
- Each backpack represents one child who died.
- Together the backpacks spell out words in Mandarin. They say, "She lived happily for seven years in this world."

10

Adrian Piper: Getting a Reaction

Adrian Margaret Smith Piper is an American artist. She was born in 1948 in New York City. Piper attended the Art Students League there. She also went to the School of Visual Arts. At school, Piper focused on painting and sculpting. But soon she was experimenting with other mediums. She was also a photographer and a filmmaker. Today, she is best known for her conceptual art.

Conceptual artists wanted to inspire thought in their viewers. Piper often did this through performance pieces. Performance art involves the artist acting in a certain way to provoke

CONCEPTUAL ART

The conceptual art movement began in the 1960s. Conceptual art is idea-based art. Artists believed that the concept, or idea, of their work is the most important thing. They do not worry about creating beautiful pieces of art. They often do not even care if their art looks like art. What they hope is that their art inspires ideas in their viewers. They want people to think about what the art means.

a response from people. As part of her *Catalysis* series, Piper once walked around with a shirt that read "Wet Paint." This caused people to wonder if the paint on her shirt was actually wet. Another time, she walked around a library playing a recording of herself belching.

Currently, Piper lives in Berlin, Germany. She runs the Adrian Piper Research Archive (APRA) Foundation Berlin. This organization works to preserve all the work that Piper has created.

7

Number of performances in Adrian Piper's *Catalysis* series

- Once, Piper soaked her clothes in vinegar and other smelly substances. Then she rode the subway.
- Another time, Piper rode the subway with a towel stuffed in her mouth.
- For one performance, Piper tied helium filled balloons to herself.

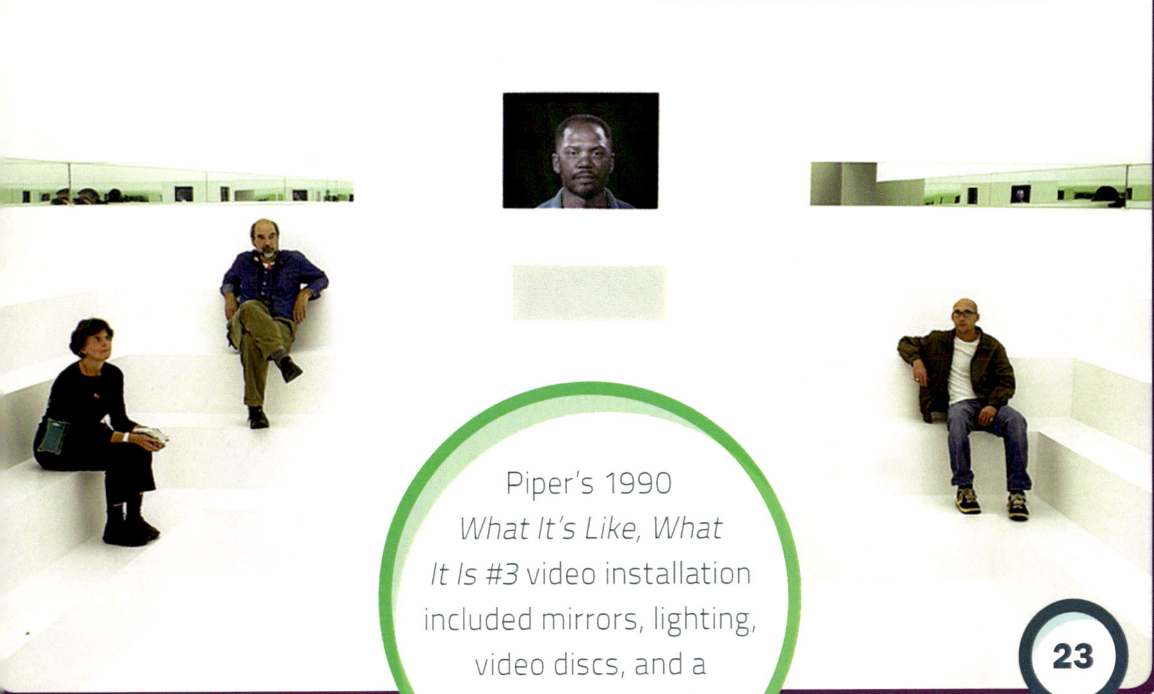

Piper's 1990 *What It's Like, What It Is #3* video installation included mirrors, lighting, video discs, and a music soundtrack.

11

Jean-Michel Basquiat: From Street Art to Fine

Jean-Michel Basquiat was an American painter. He was born in Brooklyn, New York, in 1960. Basquiat had a troubled youth. His parents divorced when he was young. His mother suffered from mental illness. In his late teens, he dropped out of school and left home. He lived on the streets with friends. Often, they stayed in abandoned buildings.

Basquiat and his friends covered the places they lived with graffiti. At the time, street art was becoming wildly popular. Graffiti artists painted colorful images on the walls of buildings and on subway trains.

Basquiat was able to transfer his street art to the canvas. He not only painted, but he used crayons to create his art. His style was extremely expressive and bold with its colors. Basquiat often placed

Jean-Michel Basquiat at his New York gallery opening in 1987.

GRAFFITI ART

Modern graffiti art began in the 1960s. It was a type of street art. Young people wrote their names, or tags, on buildings and trains. At first, they used black markers and spray paint. Over time, they added color to their tags. Their art became more elaborate and stylistic. It began to look like real art. Today, some street art sells for hundreds of thousands of dollars.

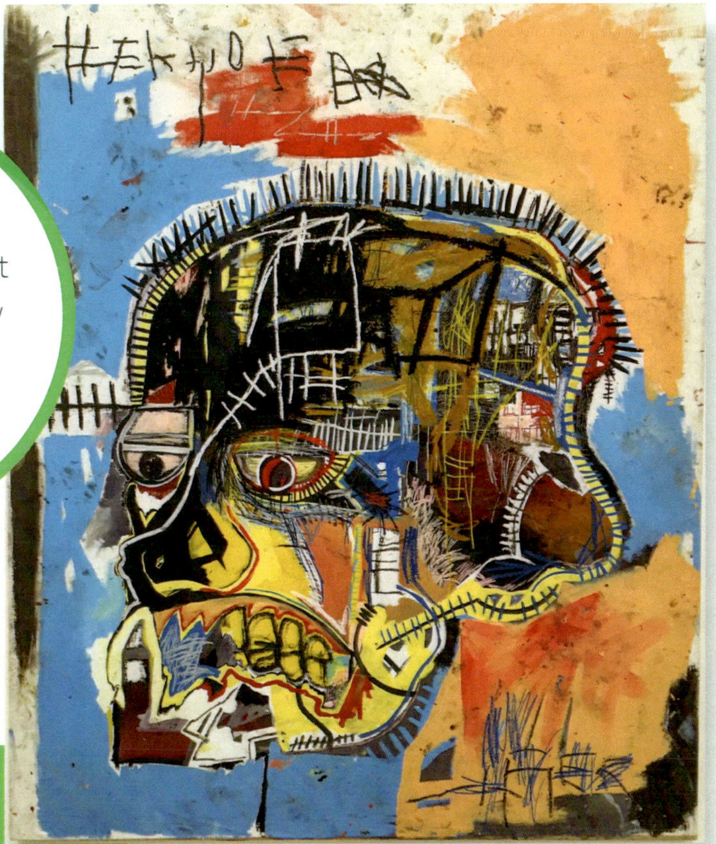

Untitled, painted by Jean-Michel Basquiat in 1981, is on display at The Broad Art Museum in California.

27
Basquiat's age when he died

- The painting *Riding with Death* was one of the last pieces of art Basquiat created.
- Basquiat was one of the few successful artists who did not go to school to study art.
- Pop artist Andy Warhol befriended Basquiat. The two made several pieces of art together.

African American figures in his art. He painted and drew *Horn Players* as well as a *Boxer*.

Basquiat's art quickly made him a celebrity. Soon, he was showing his art at museums. He appeared on the covers of magazines. Basquiat died in 1988 of an accidental drug overdose. Since then, several movies have been made about his life.

12

Banksy: Artist Anonymous

Little is known about British artist Banksy. That is not even his real name. He was born sometime in the 1970s and grew up somewhere in England. He has kept his identity secret. Banksy is a graffiti, or street, artist. He paints on the walls in public places. Many people think what he does is vandalism, not art.

Banksy's style is different than most other graffiti artists. They paint freehand. They do not use sketches or outlines as they work. Banksy uses stencils for much of his art. He cuts out designs from sheets of paper. He holds a stencil against a wall. Then he sprays paint over it.

People viewing *Girl with Balloon* after it was shredded.

$1,400,000

What Banksy's *Girl with Balloon* sold for at auction

- Banksy's early art often included animals, like rats and apes.
- He painted *Rage, Flower Thrower* on a wall in Jerusalem, Israel. It shows a masked rioter throwing flowers instead of a bomb.
- Banksy's *Girl with Balloon* now has a new name. It is *Love Is in the Bin.*

THINK ABOUT IT

Artists like Banksy use their art to make comments on social issues. Do you feel artists should use their talents to make political statements? Why or why not?

When he pulls the stencil away, a design is left on the wall. Using stencils is much quicker than painting freehand.

Banksy's work often comments on issues of the day. It is also filled with humor. In 2009, he painted a message on a bridge in London. It read "I Don't Believe in Global Warming." The words "Global Warming" were partially underwater.

Banksy is also known for his outrageous stunts. In 2018, a framed version of his *Girl with Balloon* was offered for sale by a major art auction house. A shredder was hidden in the frame. As soon as the painting sold, the shredder turned on and the painting self-destructed.

More Artists to Know

Michelangelo

Michelangelo di Lodovico Buonarroti Simoni (1475–1564) was an Italian sculptor and painter. Like other Renaissance artists, his ideas often came from the Bible. *David* is his large marble sculpture of a Biblical king. But his most famous works are in the Sistine Chapel in Vatican City in Rome, Italy. Michelangelo painted a large mural across the church's ceiling. It includes many Biblical scenes. Another mural, *The Last Judgment*, covers one of the walls.

Vincent van Gogh

Van Gogh (1890–1853) was a Dutch painter. He led the expressionist art movement. This style of art used jarring colors and bold brushstrokes to get an emotional response from viewers. *Starry Night* is one of van Gogh's best-known works. It is a painting of a night sky over a small village. The sky is filled with swirls of blue. The stars look like glowing balls of light.

Yayoi Kusama

A painter, sculptor, and performance artist, Yayoi Kusama was born in 1929 in Japan. She is best known for works of art that are covered in polka dots. Her early works were paintings covered in thousands of tiny marks. But she has since created large art installations. They include rooms filled with mirrors and objects in them. Everything is covered in colorful dots.

Kerry James Marshall

Born in 1955 in Birmingham, Alabama, Kerry James Marshall is a painter and sculptor. His works of art highlight the lives of modern African Americans. He often shows people doing everyday things. In *School of Beauty, School of Culture*, women are seen at a salon. *Vignette 15* shows a young couple at a park with their dog.

Glossary

abstract
An unreal representation of something.

anatomy
The study of human and animal bodies.

caricatures
Drawings of people, often with exaggerated features.

landscape
An outdoor scene.

medium
The materials an artist uses to create their art.

perspective
A method used in art to show depth and distance.

portrait
A drawing, painting, or photograph of a person.

Renaissance
The period of European history that followed the Middle Ages. The Renaissance is known as a time of great development in the arts and sciences.

vandalism
The act of damaging someone else's property.

Read More

Gruitrooy, Dr. Gerhard. *Mary Cassatt: An American Impressionist.* American Artists. Broomall, PA: Mason Crest, 2018.

Haynes, Danielle. *Claude Monet: Founder of French Impressionism.* Eye on Art. New York: Lucent Press, 2019.

Orr, Tamra B. *Leonardo da Vinci: Renaissance Genius.* Eye on Art. New York: Lucent Press, 2019.

Taylor, Charlotte. *Get to Know Andy Warhol.* New York: Enslow Publishing, 2016.

Wright, Susan. *Georgia O'Keeffe: An Eternal Spirit.* American Artists. Broomall, PA: Mason Crest, 2018.

Index

About the Author

Allan Morey grew up in central Wisconsin but now lives in St. Paul Minnesota, with his wife and two dogs, Stitch and Ty. He has written many books for children, and especially enjoys writing about sports and art.